For Aunt Jeanette, who takes the cake
—T.S.

For Betty, who knows where to find the best cakes in Paris
—A.R.

Katherine Tegen Books is an imprint of HarperCollins Publishers.

I Love Cake! Starring Rabbit, Porcupine, and Moose
Text copyright © 2016 by Tammi Sauer
Illustrations copyright © 2016 by Angela Rozelaar
All rights reserved. Manufactured in China.
No part of this book may be used or reproduced in any manner whatsoever
without written permission except in the case of brief quotations embodied in
critical articles and reviews. For information address HarperCollins Children's Books,
a division of HarperCollins Publishers, 195 Broadway, New York, NY 10007.
www.harpercollinschildrens.com
ISBN 978-0-06-227894-4

The artist used a brush and India ink and Photoshop
to create and color the digital illustrations for this book.
Typography by Rachel Zegar
16 17 18 19 20 SCP 10 9 8 7 6 5 4 3 2 1
❖
First Edition

I LOVE CAKE!

Starring Rabbit, Porcupine, and Moose

Story by **Tammi Sauer**   Pictures by **Angie Rozelaar**

 KATHERINE TEGEN BOOKS
An Imprint of HarperCollins Publishers

In the middle of Sweet Valley Woods lived Rabbit, Porcupine, and Moose.

I am Rabbit.

I am Porcupine

I am Frog.
Just kidding!
I am Moose.

And that's the way they liked it.

That's the way we like it.

One morning, Rabbit bounced
out of bed extra early.

Hooray! It's
my birthday!

She invited Porcupine and Moose to her party.

Be at my house in one hour.

Sounds fun!

CAKE!

The three friends got ready.

Rabbit grabbed her to-do list.

I love throwing parties.

Porcupine struck a party pose.

I love
playing games.

Moose squeezed into
his favorite sweater.

I love boiled turnips.
Ha! I do not. I love cake.

Porcupine and Moose tried to make it to the party on time, but . . .

Finally, they arrived at Rabbit's house.

Next they played pin the tail on the chipmunk.

Then Rabbit and Porcupine heard a mysterious noise.

Nom-nom-nom.

What was that?

But Rabbit didn't give it much thought. She had an important announcement to make.

It's time for cake!

Rabbit and Porcupine looked everywhere
for the missing cake and the missing Moose.

At last they made a big discovery.

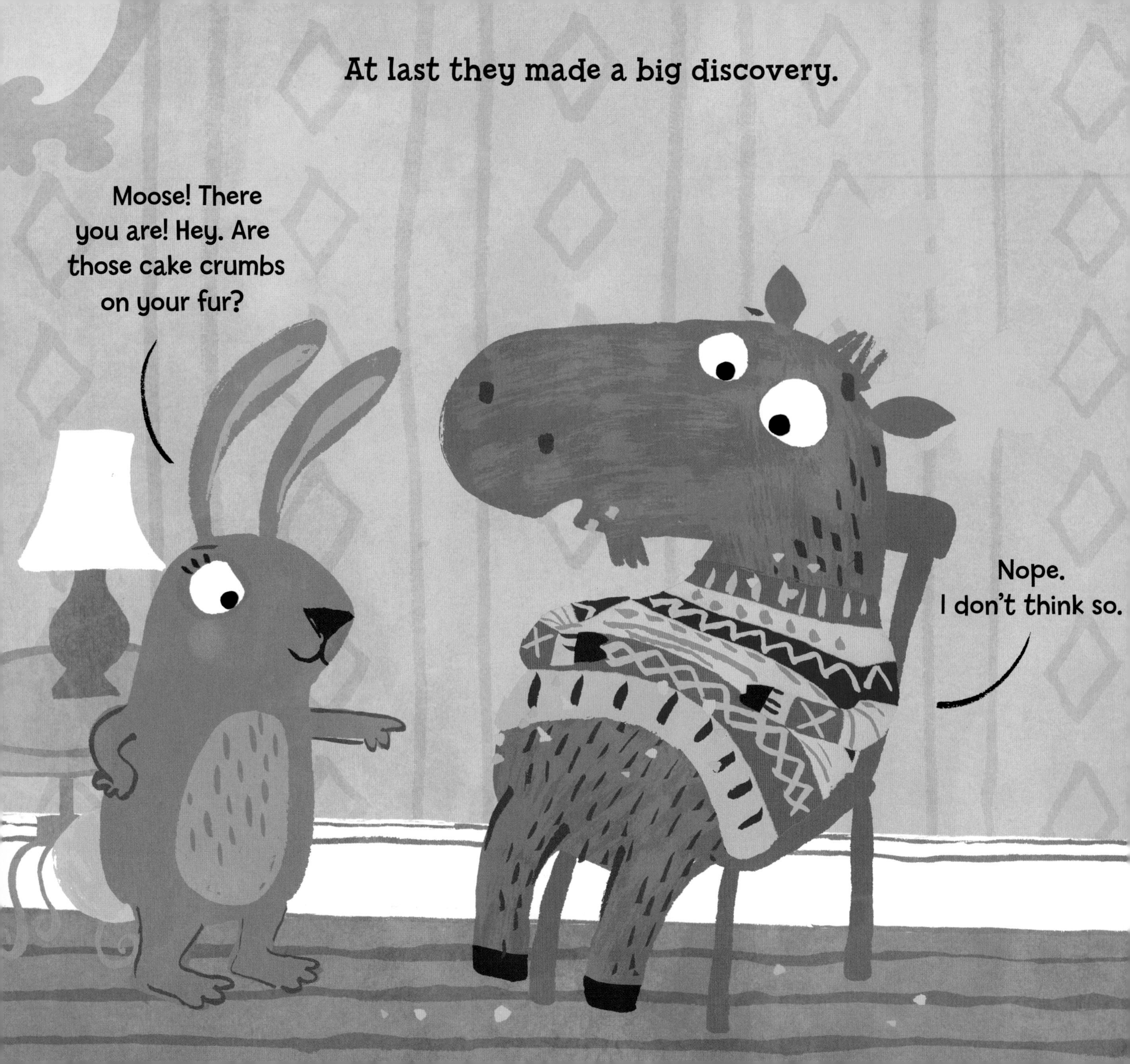

Rabbit and Porcupine gave Moose the Look.

What? You think I ate the cake? That hurts. Maybe a badger ate the cake. Did you ever think of that?

Rabbit and Porcupine only wanted one thing.
And it was gone.

All of that sniffling made Moose sniffly, too.

Awww! Why do you have to look so sweet and adorable and—?

I CAN'T TAKE IT ANY LONGER! MAYBE I HAD ONE BITE OF CAKE, BUT THAT IS ALL. I ONLY WANTED TO MAKE SURE IT WAS OKAY. THAT'S FINE, RIGHT? IS IT MY FAULT MY MOUTH'S SO BIG THAT THE WHOLE CAKE KIND OF FELL RIGHT IN? I'M REALLY SORRY. CAN WE ALL STILL BE FRIENDS? PRETTY PLEASE, I BEG YOU! WE CAN GET MATCHING SWEATERS. WHAT DO YOU SAY?

Rabbit got hopping mad.

You ruined my
whole party.

Porcupine got prickly.

This is no fun.

Moose got the message.

Back at home, Moose thought of ways to
make it up to his friends.

Flowers?

Poetry?

A singing
gorilla?

But nothing seemed quite right.

Later that day, Moose returned to Rabbit's house.

friends

SURPRISE!

Rabbit and Porcupine tried to ignore Moose.

But Moose was just so Moose.

Rabbit loved the surprise.

Porcupine loved the surprise.

Moose loved the surprise exactly
as much as he loved cake.

I love cake!
But . . .

THE END